PHILOMEL BOOKS
An imprint of Penguin Random House LLC, New York

First published in the United States of America by Philomel Books,
an imprint of Penguin Random House LLC, 2022

Text copyright © 2022 by Drew Daywalt
Illustrations copyright © 2022 by Oliver Jeffers

Philomel Books is a registered trademark of
Penguin Random House LLC.

Visit us online at penguinrandomhouse.com.

Library of Congress Cataloging-in-Publication Data is available.

Manufactured in China

ISBN 9780593353387

10 9 8 7 6 5 4 3

Edited by Jill Santopolo
Design by Rory Jeffers
Text set in Mercury.

Art was created with gouache, ink, colored pencil, and crayon.

GREEN
IS FOR
CHRISTMAS

ACTUALLY, RED IS FOR CHRISTMAS, BUT please tell ME more.

DREW DAYWALT
OLIVER JEFFERS

PHILOMEL

GREEN
IS FOR
CHRISTMAS

GREEN
IS FOR
HOLLY

A hem!

RED

IS FOR

CHRISTMAS

RED

IS FOR

candy
canes

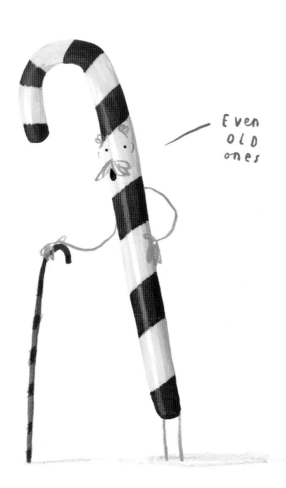

Even
OLD
ones

GREEN
is For
FiR
TREES

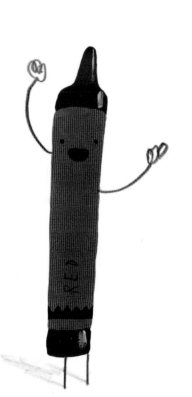

RED

IS FOR

SANTA

CLAUS

DARN
Right
IT IS!

Listen, you guys,
I'm INVISible
ALL YEAR long,
so you're NOT
TAKing this one
AWAY from ME.

HELLO!

Snowflakes?
SNOWMEN?
MARSHMallows?

WHITE

is for

christmas

I'm kind of a **BIG DEAL** on the CHRISTMAS TREE

HELLO!

SILVER is FOR CHRISTMAS

WHAT'S CHRISTMAS
WITHOUT
SILVER BELLS?

You JUST TRY
jingling
WITHOUT ME!

I'm not sure
why I'm here,
but YEAH!
What HE said.

what about cookies
and REINDEER?

BROWN
IS FOR
CHRISTmas

I'm more
Burnt Sienna,
but that's cool!

HUH?

'TIS the
SEASON TO
BE JOLLY
TRA LA LA LA LA

YOU CAN'T HAVE

WITHOUT   ANY

CHRISTMAS

OF US.

Nice HAT

Especially
green!